"I think that these books are well-written. I also
think that these books are good for all ages."
Logan Volpe, age 12

"I love it when books I read make me think.
In this book I felt like I was the one solving the
problems. I also liked the different endings."
Lainey Curtis, age 10

"I think these books are cool because
you actually get involved in them."
Melanie Armstrong, age 12

"So many places to go from dying to
winning a battle or race. You get to be
the author and choose how it ends!"
Brooks Curran, age 11

THE ISLAND OF TIME

BY R. A. MONTGOMERY

COVER AND INTERIOR ILLUSTRATED BY
MARCO CANNELLA

sundance™

The Island of Time ©1991 R. A. Montgomery
Warren, Vermont. All Rights Reserved.

Artwork, design, and revised text © 2006 Chooseco LLC,
Warren, Vermont. All Rights Reserved.

Illustrated by: Marco Cannella
Book design: Stacey Hood, Big Eyedea Visual Design

For information regarding permission, write to:

A Haights Cross Communications ꞏ Company

Sundance Publishing
P.O. Box 740
One Beeman Road
Northborough, MA 01532-0740
800-343-8204
www.sundancepub.com

ISBN-13: 978-1-4207-0311-5
ISBN-10: 1-4207-0311-0

Published simultaneously in the United States and Canada

Printed in China

BEWARE and WARNING!

This book is different from other books.

You and YOU ALONE are in charge of what happens in this story.

There are dangers, choices, adventures, and consequences. YOU must use all of your numerous talents and much of your enormous intelligence. The wrong decision could end in disaster—even death. But, don't despair. At any time, YOU can go back and make another choice, alter the path of your story, and change its result.

A stormy day on Lake Champlain has set you off course. You and your friend Jayme were attempting to reach Providence Island, where your family has a cabin. Now you're trapped in a storm in open water, with just your small inflatable motorboat and a few paddles. This storm has changed more than your travel plans, though. Something very suspicious is happening all around you. You've heard legends and stories about this area, from Champ the lake monster to some mysterious Indian burial mounds. You may have gone back in time! Will you meet with the tribes who lived here centuries ago, or visit an antiquated historical hotel the day before it burned to the ground? Only you can decide!

You've been given a lucky break. Once a year you get a day off from school so your teachers can catch up on their administrative paperwork. The timing is perfect. The day falls on a Friday, and your parents are away on a business trip. They are architects, and they have a client in New Mexico who wants to build an environmentally sound solar house. To ensure this, they had to go and look at the site. Much to your delight, they have left you all alone for the first time. For a year and a half now you've been trying to convince them that they could.

"Mom, I'm old enough now. Trust me. I can look after my sister. I'm reliable," was your standard speech. However, this time things were different. You didn't even have to ask.

"We're going out of town for a few days," your mom said. "We'll be in New Mexico, and your father and I have decided—"

Before she could finish, you blurted out, "Oh, no. You're not gonna have some drip move in here to take care of me and Devon, are you? That's a fate worse than death."

"Are you listening?" your mother asked.

"Sure, Mom, you were saying?"

"Well, if you're not really interested, I can make other arrangements."

"What do you mean?" you asked hesitantly, panic setting in slowly.

Turn to page 3.

2

Lantern pricks up his ears and begins to howl.

"You feel something, too?" Jayme says to Lantern. "It's spooky. It feels like there's someone else here."

Lantern gives another haunting howl. It reverberates within the high ceiling and its pine beams. It sends chills up your spine. You don't like this one bit.

You've got to do something, you realize. You're still alive, you know that; they can sense you. You've got to bring yourself back from wherever you are.

With extraordinary concentration and willpower, you force yourself to materialize in front of Jayme and Lantern. You have no idea what you are doing, or how, but somehow it works!

"It's you!" Jayme cries, taken aback by your sudden appearance. "We gave you up for dead. But where'd you come from? Where have you been?"

Turn to page 33.

"Your father and I have arranged for your sister to stay with Belinda Grist," your mother said. "You know her, my old friend from Dayton, Ohio."

Your spirits tumbled. Belinda Grist was far and away Number One on your hate list.

And then she finished. "You are to stay home—alone. That is, if you want to."

For a moment you remained quiet as the full meaning of the announcement hit you. Then you were flooded with excitement. Trying to sound like an adult, you replied as calmly as possible, "Well, given the circumstances, I would be only too . . . uh . . . happy to do this for you, Mom."

Your mother gave you a knowing look. For just a moment you feared that the deal was off, and that you would be condemned to spend the time with the dreaded Ms. Belinda Grist. But you were wrong.

"Good, then it's settled. Water the plants, feed the dog, and take messages—the answering machine is on the fritz again," your mother instructed. "Oh, and don't forget to recycle bottles, cans, and papers. I'll leave the number where we'll be on the refrigerator. You can always get in touch with Belinda or Charlie Munson if you need to. But of course you won't, right?"

"Right."

Turn to the next page.

4

That was two days ago. And what freedom it's been! You've stayed up late watching all nine hundred channels of satellite cable; you've eaten pizza every meal; you've forgotten to brush your teeth, on purpose; and you've even worn the same clothes two days in a row. This must be what it's like to be as rich as royalty, you think. You even have a loyal subject, Lantern, your dog, who waits at your beck and call.

Friday, your day off from school, has finally arrived. "What should I do?" you ask yourself. You don't like to sleep late. And hanging around the house, which is pretty isolated, can be boring.

"I've got it!" you announce to Lantern, who sits anxiously at your feet waiting for a strip of bacon. Lantern will eat anything. He's your dependable garbage disposal and four-legged trash can. "We'll go to Providence Island. How about that?" you say, giving him another strip and slapping him playfully on his snout. Lantern gives you a kind of nervous yawn, a cross between a question and a squashed yip. He likes the bacon, but you're not so sure about the announcement.

At that moment the telephone rings. You hate telephones; they always interrupt what you're doing. You think about not answering it, but then you remember your mother's instructions. And yet, if you just let it ring, who will know?

If you decide to answer it, turn to page 85.

If you decide to ignore the phone, turn to page 14.

10

"I don't like the looks of this," Jayme says. "I think we're in for a big storm. Look over there!" She points west. The mountains are gone, covered by white and gray clouds and mist. The wind is whistling, getting stronger, and the temperature has fallen.

You look back toward the dock, but you can barely make it out any longer. The shoreline is dim and indistinct. In a matter of minutes the waves have mounted to four or five feet.

A monster wave bashes its way over the port side of the boat, swamping the shallow space that holds the gas can and daypacks you and Jayme have brought along. You slow the boat down in an attempt to deal with each wave as safely as possible. Unfortunately, the automatic bailing doesn't work too well at this speed. Water sloshes in the Zodiac, tinged with the rainbow colors of the spilled gas and oil.

"Let's head back!" Jayme shouts, her voice thin in the midst of rushing wind and the growl of the motor.

Your instinct tells you she's right. However, you are more than halfway to the island. Perhaps you should continue on ahead and seek shelter there.

If you decide to turn around and go back to the dock, turn to page 83.

If you decide to go on, turn to page 34.

Yikes! You're falling!

Your scream echoes in the empty space that surrounds you. The speed of your fall accelerates as you tumble in space for what seems like forever. A warm wind begins to envelop you, pushing up against you. It creates the same effect as a parachute would.

You continue to fall until you feel your body slow down. Gradually you come to land on a grassy slope. It is now light out, the sun slipping behind the edge of a range of mountains. The area looks familiar, but there is something odd about it.

Where am I? you wonder. You feel your arms and legs and check for bruises or broken bones, surprised to find none.

"Hello," you shout. "Can anybody hear me?"

Standing up, you see a ridge covered with birch trees. There seems to be some kind of clearing behind them. The sounds of chanting and music come faintly from that direction.

Turn to page 87.

Without waiting for your answer, the four people escort you over to the amphitheater. The singing and chanting have now stopped, but the silence that fills the air is charged with joy and wonder.

A tall figure moves to the center of the amphitheater. He spreads his arms out as if to embrace all those present. He is adorned by the feathers of the great horned owl.

"Oh, Great Spirit, we give thanks for the life you have given us. We that walk and crawl and swim and fly recognize the greatness of the life force. We ask for your guidance and protection."

With a calm and deliberate motion, the figure moves to a huge pile of brush in the center of the clearing. A young boy and a girl approach him, handing him a lighted torch. With this torch, he fires the great pile of brush. It bursts into flame just as the sun sinks behind the far hills and mountains. A joyous chant rises out of the group that has assembled, giving thanks for life and praying for guidance.

Suddenly you are sent whirling back through the darkness, ascending the vertical funnel with the same speed as your fall. The chanting grows fainter and fainter but remains with you as you complete your journey.

Turn to page 84.

14

Deciding to ignore the phone, you get lucky—two more rings and the phone stops. Good, you think. I've got bigger and better things to do today.

You live in northern Vermont, not too far from Lake Champlain. Champlain is huge as far as lakes go. It's about 125 miles long, quite wide, and runs into Canada on its northern end. It's beautiful, with the Green Mountains to the east and the Adirondack Mountains to the west, their rugged stone covered with pine, hemlock, and birch.

On the lake about eight miles away, your family has a dock that belongs to Providence Island. Your family has owned property on Providence Island for quite a few years. The island is big, over 160 acres in size, and a mile and a half long. It's situated in the widest part of the lake. When you're out there, it almost feels like you're on a different planet. It's really special, really isolated. Some people say that the past is alive there.

The dock stretches out into the lake in a big L. It was built years ago, and time has not been kind to it. Ice, water, and the pounding of waves have all gnawed away at it, leaving raw-looking concrete wounds in its foundation.

Turn to the next page.

16

Off to the side, there is a small boathouse. That's where the family boat is kept—a 13-foot inflatable Zodiac. It's red, and if there is only one person onboard, it can go really fast. Your dad says it's one of the safest boats on the lake. You believe him, but in rough weather, the waves come right over the bow, soaking you. But that's part of the fun. Your boat can take anything the lake has to dish out, and sometimes that can be plenty.

The prevailing winds are the westerlies. The lake sits in between the two mountain ranges, and when the wind swoops down off the Adirondacks, zooming over the lake, it hits the Greens in Vermont, where it shifts direction and frequently roars back up the lake from the south.

Turn to page 72.

You are on familiar ground once again. Your parents' summer house looms ahead of you through the pine and cedar trees. For a moment you look back, trying to find the light and recapture its comfort; but it is gone. Regret fills your heart. You were given an opportunity, and you let it slip away. With a heavy heart you run for the house. The lights are on in the living room and the smell of wood smoke coming from the fireplace hangs in the air.

"Jayme! Lantern! It's me. I'm back," you yell. "You won't believe where I've been."

You begin to explain, then stop yourself. Perhaps it's best not to speak about it until you've had some time to think about this experience.

The End

18

"How's it coming?" Jayme shouts, her voice barely audible against the wind. Despite the fact that there is a good four inches of lake water in the bottom of the Zodiac, she has taken refuge from the waves there, sharing the space with Lantern, who seems less than pleased.

"No problem. We're heading back. Hang in there," you advise, despite your own fear.

The combination of wind, fog, and rain have all begun to distort your sense of direction. You're having a difficult time. The Zodiac is turning in a slow and sloppy arc.

The wind increases. You estimate its gusts at 40 knots or more.

"Where am I?" you ask yourself. "Okay, calm down, don't worry, the clouds will lift. Just stay calm."

"What's wrong?" Jayme asks.

"Oh, nothing. I was just saying that I think we should put on our life vests. Okay?"

"I've already got mine on. We're lost, aren't we?"

"Well, not really. I mean, we're on the lake. We can't be too far from land. It's not like we're out in the ocean."

"I knew I shouldn't have come. Why do I let you talk me into things?"

"Jayme, calm down. We're not in trouble. We're going to be all right. Just trust me." It is at that precise moment that the motor coughs, kicks, sputters, and dies.

Turn to page 91.

The couple look up, somewhat surprised to see you waving and shouting at them. They wave back. "Sure, the more the merrier," the man replies.

You call to Jayme and Lantern, then race down the path to the rocky beach, where they pick up everyone in their dinghy.

As you tell them the story of your day on the island, you hear the sound of the black powerboat. It's roaring up the lake toward Canada.

When you return home, you notify your parents and the authorities. Mr. Stilton is wanted for embezzlement, it turns out; but neither he nor Ludwig are ever heard from again.

The End

20

You are sorry to see them go, but you are intrigued by your situation and the world you have somehow fallen into.

You notice a paper on one of the deck chairs. It is a copy of the *New York Globe* dated July 9, 1890. You have barely time to look when First Officer Kelly commands, "I need you up here."

You fold up the paper and stick it in your back pocket. Then you mount the forward stairs to the bridge where Kelly stands by the engine room controls.

"Something strange is going on, youngster. We've had a little trouble onboard. The captain, who's a good judge of character, seems to think you're to be trusted. So, I want you to go ashore. Go up to the hotel and see what you can find out," Kelly says, looking you in the eye.

"About what?" you ask, perplexed at your assignment.

Turn to page 53.

"That was close!" you say to Lantern, who seems to be hoping for more bacon.

Then the telephone rings again. This time you refuse to answer it. Let it ring, you say to yourself.

You laugh, enjoying the power you have over the phone. What nerve, you think, proud of yourself.

On the other end of the telephone line is a disc jockey from WKYB radio in the North Country. "Well, so much for our million-dollar winner! As you know, once every six months, ladies and gentlemen, we pick a number at random and make one, and only one, call. If our lucky winner names WKYB as their favorite radio station, they win our million-dollar prize. Well, it looks like there's nobody home. We'll try again in six months. But for now, have a nice day out there in the North Country."

In a way, it's a good thing you'll never know who called.

The End

22

"What the heck," you say. "A few more minutes isn't going to hurt anyone." Your decision made, you begin to investigate the cave. For a fleeting moment you look around you, taking in everything as if for the last time. Somehow you know that once you enter, your life will never be the same again. It isn't danger or fear that you feel; rather, it is a sense that beyond the entrance lie the answers to some of life's riddles, answers known ages ago but long since forgotten by the human race in its greed-driven rush for growth and success.

The moment of reflection passes. With the sun breaking from behind the clouds, the forest, the mounds, and the rocks take on a golden hue. You step into a ray of sunlight that illuminates the entrance and commit yourself to your decision to seek out what lies beyond. You squeeze between the dark, sharp rocks and enter the cave.

The darkness extends before you, creating a barrier. The floor is covered with dry leaves and pine needles. There is a scurrying sound as some small creature makes off for its safety. You stand still, trying to fight your fears, letting your eyes adjust to the darkness. Slowly it recedes, and you can vaguely discern the immediate area before you. Cautiously you move forward.

Turn to page 11.

"Jayme, you're not going to like this, but I think we should try and swim for shore," you say.

"No, no way! I've had enough of your schemes. You're going to get us killed," she says, looking at Lantern for support

Lantern looks up at you blankly, his fur matted and wet.

"Now hold on. We don't have much time. Let me try and explain—"

Before you get a chance to finish your sentence, Lantern shifts his position in the boat, causing Jayme to fall overboard into the lake. Grabbing Lantern by his collar, you jump over the side of the Zodiac, treading water alongside Jayme.

Turn to page 103.

You, Jayme, and Lantern stroll leisurely down the broad path, taking everything in, giving in to the summery weather and the smell of pines and cedar.

Near the middle of the island, you come across a tennis court and a croquet lawn, where women in long dresses and men wearing white flannel pants and long-sleeved shirts are playing. They don't seem to notice you.

As a matter of fact, when you look at Jayme, you hardly notice her either. You are surprised to see only an outline, not much more than a shadow walking along the path. Lantern too is just a yellowish blur. Looking down at your hands, you see a silvery glow, but no real human form.

"Whoa, what's happening?" you ask as panic sets in.

"Where are you?" Jayme shouts, looking around for you. "Where'd you go?"

"I'm right here, don't worry. Something's happened to us, but I'm not sure what."

Turn to page 8.

"It won't be long now," the man continues, filling your cups with more tea.

You have no idea who this old man is, or what he is talking about. Alien or not, the man lives in a cave—you have to wonder about his sanity.

"Do you wish to come along?" he asks with a smile.

"No, thanks," you say gracefully, looking at Jayme. "All we want is to get away from some people who were chasing us outside the cave." You look around anxiously, fearing that your voices will lead the woodsman and the others from the boat down into the cave.

"Not to worry," the old man says. "I put the shield back in place after the three of you entered the cave. The entrance is no longer visible to the outside world. You are safe now. Please, stay with me awhile. I have much to tell you."

You look at Jayme. Like you, she seems to question the man and his story. But he seems harmless enough. With a shrug, you decide to hear him out.

Later that day, you and Jayme leave the cave and carefully make your way to the west side of the island. The storm is over, and the lake is calming down. The big cruiser has disappeared. All you have to do now is wait to be rescued.

The End

"Time is running out," the voice warns you. It seems to come from higher in the air now, as if it were all around you. Slowly you remove your grip on the birch branch and move forward.

You want to scream to Jayme and Lantern for help, but you are also strangely drawn by the voice.

"Follow me," the voice calls to you.

As tempted as you are to follow, caution, on the other hand, dictates that you break away and head for the woods.

If you follow the voice, turn to page 108.

If you break away, turn to page 35.

"Hey, you kids! Don't you know this is no day for a swim," a voice shouts from the boat.

Moments later, you, Jayme, and Lantern are pulled aboard by a burly man and his wife. The heated cabin is more than comforting, and the hot cocoa hits the spot.

After telling them your story, you think about the Zodiac and worry about how you're ever going to explain to your dad what happened. In your heart you know you did all you could. If you hadn't abandoned ship and swum for shore, you might still be out in the broad center of the lake, drifting along in a boat without a motor.

"Well," you say to Jayme, "things could have been a lot worse. At the very least we had some excitement on our day off."

Jayme looks at you as if you are out of your mind. Your poor friend's been through enough. You decide to let it go for now.

The End

The   Chini

Looking around you, you realize you are no longer on Providence Island. The pines are gone, as are the birches. These trees are different; they bulge out horizontally, balloonlike and enormous. They must be over two hundred feet tall! Their leaves are larger than your hand; the color green more intense than any you've seen.

Above the trees the sky is completely clear. Sunlight falls gently through the branches and the leaves. It is now warm and summery. You shed your wet windbreaker and continue to move forward, walking on what appears to be a carpet of flowers.

Turn to page 47.

32

"Not like we have much choice, do we?" Jayme says to you with a look of disgust.

Suddenly a monster wave engulfs the boat. Before you have time to think or react, the Zodiac washes up on some huge slabs of rock. You hear a tear as the bottom of the Zodiac drags along the bottom and rips open.

"We made it! We made it!" you shout, scrambling out of the wounded boat and onto shore. You do your best to try and drag the boat up onto the rocks and out of the water, but the task, even with Jayme, is difficult. You hear another whooshing sound as the starboard compartment is ripped open by the rocky shore. "Grab the packs," you shout.

Good old Lantern, you notice, has the straps of one of the backpacks in his mouth. He scrambles onto the rocks and with a bound is up on the bank.

A row of tall pine trees forms a backdrop. Together they look like a fortress, with the clouds seeming to form a gray roof above them.

Turn to page 76.

Lantern's howl turns into a happy yelp, as he jumps on you and paws you playfully.

It feels good to be back, and you want to tell Jayme all that you have been through since you split up, but for now you decide to rest. "It's been a long day. I'll tell you everything later," you say.

Jayme goes back to the telephone and calls the Coast Guard and the state police.

"Everything's all right," she says. "I've found our friend. Now all we need is a way off this island."

Jayme breathes a sigh of relief. They should be coming for the three of you soon. But something tells you that you're not out of the water yet, so to speak. You still have a lot of explaining to do. And after what happened to the Zodiac, your parents aren't going to buy any stories about voices, Indian burial mounds, or pulling yourself back from the dead. You can't blame them, either.

The End

"Hang on, we're more than halfway there," you call to Jayme above the sounds of the motor and wind. "It's not that bad, really. Just think of the stories we can tell back in school. You know, heroes of the lake, stuff like that." As much as you try and reassure Jayme, you yourself are worried. The water is rough, but you should make it, you convince yourself.

Jayme holds on to Lantern, the two of them staring with uncertainty on their faces.

A vicious gust of wind and water smacks you in the face. It makes you really angry. But then, how can you get angry at the lake? Smack! It happens again.

"Okay, that does it!" you shout to the wind and the waves.

Grasping the handle of the motor, you apply more power, feeling the red Zodiac chew into the black water. A foam of white curls past the bow, then drops off, leaving behind a barely discernible path in the water. Fog drifts by, swallowing you in its grip.

"Turn back!" Jayme shouts, hiding from the full force of the waves by crouching next to Lantern on the floor of the boat.

"It's too late. Hold on," you reply, trying to steady the boat.

The fog shifts a little, and you realize that you are near the south end of the island, way off course.

What are you going to do?

Turn to page 110.

An inner strength emerges from within you and helps you to break away from the hypnotic effect of the voice. Your sense of survival returns, and you decide to run, to get as far away from the voice as possible.

"Wait, don't go. This is your destiny," the voice cries, its lingering, sweet tone trying to lure you back.

You look back over your shoulder to see if you are being followed, when, whomp! You smash into a towering pine tree.

Lying on the ground, you feel for bruises but seem to be okay. A momentary nausea overcomes you. You manage to push it aside, scramble to your feet, and push on.

The going is rough. Although you know the island really well, with the fog and the rain you have become disoriented and do not recognize the area at all.

The voice has stopped. The forest is now silent and seems more remote than ever. You stand there perfectly still, concentrating with all your might. All is silent. There is nothing around except for the trees and the sound of an occasional drip from a needled bough.

Turn to page 68.

"Okay, now squirm your way over to my voice," you say.

"Yikes! Bugs!" Jayme calls with alarm.

Then you see her at the edge of the house, clawing desperately at the lattice that covers the gap between the floor and the cellar area. The house is built on old wooden piers. You help her, wrenching the lattice free.

"Where are those guys? I didn't hear a sound," Jayme says, getting to her feet.

"Me neither," you reply. "Not now, anyway."

Go on to the next page.

Lantern comes up from behind and gives your hand a lick. You nearly jump out of your skin.

"It's only you," you say, looking down at the happy face of your dog.

"Let's make tracks and get out of here," Jayme says. "I say we head to the West Cove."

"Sounds as good a plan as any," you agree.

The three of you skirt the house and make it to the West Cove, looking over your shoulder for thugs hiding in the woods.

"Hold up!" you whisper urgently. "I hear something."

"Oh, no, what now?" Jayme asks dejectedly.

Turn to page 63.

38

"Those men were my, uh, business partners," Stilton says nervously. "We had some special dealings."

You cast a disapproving look. "I don't believe you," you say in your best, most authoritative voice.

Stilton looks dejectedly at the ground. "I might as well confess," he says. "Maybe the authorities will go easier on me.

"I'm an embezzler. There's a warrant out for my arrest. We were headed for Canada in that boat," he admits. "We got caught in the storm, otherwise we would have made it."

"As soon as we get off the island we can notify the police," you say optimistically. "I'm sure they'll go easy on you for tipping them off."

You and Jayme exchange glances, looking at the now-pathetic figure of Mr. Stilton. You feel sorry for him, but you know justice must run its course.

The End

The waves are beginning to get enormous. Without a motor, you are at the mercy of the storm and the lake.

A radical thought now crosses your mind. Maybe, just maybe, you would be better off abandoning ship and swimming for shore. It can't be far. You just might stand a better chance of surviving than if you remained on board the Zodiac, drifting at the mercy of the waves.

No doubt about it—it's a risky plan. But if you are going to swim, you'd better start now. Once you reach the broad center of the lake, swimming will be futile.

If you decide to swim for the island, turn to page 23.

If you decide to stay with the Zodiac, turn to page 96.

40

Lantern howls weakly. You are touched by their sadness and wish you could do something to let them know you're okay. You try again.

"Hey, you guys, look, it's me. I'm not dead. Wake up!" you say. You have no idea what's going on, or what could have happened to you. It must have something to do with the strange voice you encountered earlier in the forest, you speculate.

Turn to page 2.

42

Lantern settles down, nuzzling the old man's hand. You and Jayme sink to the floor of the cave, sitting cross-legged.

The old man pours a steaming brew of tea that smells of flowers and herbs. You take a cup, sip, and relax as your fears subside and you forget the world outside.

"A long, long time ago," the old man begins, "on a planet very much like this one, there lived a group of scientists. One day they launched out to explore the cosmos. Some landed here on this planet. I was with those explorers. The others have gone farther into this cave, seeking the source of its multi-dimensions and passages into time and beyond. I chose to stay here and conduct my experiments in this dimension, at this point in time. Now I wait for transport to come and take me back home."

Turn to page 26.

Getting down is easier for you than going up. When you reach terra firma you quickly head for the rocks, only to find them slippery with moss and damp from the rain.

For fifteen minutes you circle them, looking for an opening or a clue to something—anything. And then you find it, a slit big enough for one person to squeeze through, leading to a cave of some kind. You peer into the darkness, testing the silence with a half-shout.

"Anybody there?" you yell, knowing there won't be any answer. And of course there isn't.

Turn to page 73.

44

Deciding to try and take control of their boat, you slip into the water, shocked at how cold it is.

"Wow, maybe this is a really dumb idea," you say to Lantern, who is paddling along beside you. You swim with the quietest of strokes over to the boat.

Moments later you are at the side of the black hull. Reaching up, you grab hold of the boarding ladder, only to find yourself on the other end of a gun. You are bound, gagged, and deposited roughly on the exposed dock.

The black-hulled boat departs, its motors grumbling in the heavy air. It takes you quite a while to loosen the knots. Some day off this has been!

The End

"You are here with us," the figure replies. "Remember, things are not always what they may appear to be. You and I now occupy the same space at the same time. You are the present; we are both the future and the past."

The figure shifts its position, changing its form into a rainbow. Lantern's barking grows louder.

"I must be dreaming," you say, shaking your head. "Either that or I'm on a movie set."

"You must not question the experience. You have been given a rare chance. You have been given the opportunity to see the future.

"Time can be a difficult concept to grasp. That understanding will come with age. You shall see. Perhaps you are not ready yet. Come, I will guide you back to that which you know. Follow me."

The light takes a human form again. It rises up over the forest, leaving a trail. You follow as if in a trance. Gone now is your hostility, your doubts and fatigue. You feel an exhilaration inside, the way you do after completing a long run or winning a championship game.

The light begins to fade, and its voice, once calm and soothing, is now silent.

Turn to page 17.

The voice slowly drops from the trees, settles to the ground, and begins to materialize in front of you. At first it is just a golden light, not unlike a Fourth of July sparkler. Then it begins to take on a more definite shape, more otherworldly than human. From the center of the mass the light intensifies, changing from golden to silver to a whitish hue.

For a moment you feel tense; a part of you wishes to turn back and escape.

"Don't be afraid," the voice says, comforting you. "This is just the beginning."

Your heart is beating fast, you realize, but you steel yourself to be calm as you continue to experience this unknown.

Turn to page 49.

48

"Hey, you two!" a sailor in a blue uniform shouts at you and Jayme. "Want a job?"

"You mean us?" you reply.

"I don't mean your dog—that is, unless he's a talking dog. Of course I mean you. We're short-handed, and we need to add to our crew. Can't get good help these days, you know how it is. You young people. . . . Well, they don't raise them the way they used to," he says, blustering on and on.

"What kind of work?" you ask curiously. Then it dawns on you: why doesn't he say anything about the strange boat you and Jayme are in? If you really are in the past, and this is not part of some joke or a film production, then he would have noticed your modern boat by now. Well, whatever's responsible for this turn of events, perhaps it causes him to see everything as it is in his own time period. Maybe he sees you and Jayme dressed in nineteenth-century clothing and your boat as a wooden skiff.

"We can use a hand with mostly everything on the boat; everything short of being captain, that is. You can handle lines, carry luggage, stand watch, even be the wiper in the engine room. It's good fun. Doesn't pay much, but you'll get a lot of experience." He then smiles at the two of you, waiting for your reply.

Turn to page 97.

"You are brave," the voice reassures you.

The shining light form now condenses, resting before you upon a tuft of grass.

In the distance you hear a mournful howl.

"Lantern?" you ask as the howl repeats itself.

"Keep focused," the figure guides you. "Clear your mind."

Something tugs at you to follow the sound of Lantern's howl and break away from this spell.

You make an attempt, finding it difficult to return yet not impossible. You have the feeling you could free yourself if you wanted to.

However, there's also a strong part of you that wants to discover what is in store for you.

The sound of Lantern's howl grows fainter. If you are going to retreat, you'll have to do it now.

If you decide to break away, turn to page 80.

If you stay where you are, turn to page 59.

50

"It leads outside from under the house," you tell Jayme. "Just crawl along until you get to the outside wall. Then we'll figure out a way to escape."

"We almost got killed," she says with exasperation in her voice. "What do we do? We've got to get out of here. We've got to get home."

"Hang in there. We'll be fine. Just find the trap-door," you reply.

By now, the sun has replaced the clouds in the sky. At least the weather's picked up.

"Hey, I can't find it," Jayme says, her voice muffled by the narrow passageway.

"It's there. Keep looking," you say, glancing around to see if anyone is coming.

"I found it!" Jayme says moments later in triumph. "It's heavy."

Turn to page 36.

"Granted there were some tribes in this area that were pretty warlike," your grandfather continued. "The Mohawks, for example. But the Indians around here like the Abenakis were friendly. They minded their own business. It's been said that Providence Island was an important place for them, a ceremonial island where they came to celebrate the harvest and the hunt. Some say that it was also a healing island—that when the elders were sick or wounded, they were brought here to recover or to prepare for their journey into the next world. Those mounds over on the north end are their graves. Some say that the spirits of the Indians buried here have never left; they roam the land looking for the past, hoping to find a path to lead them off the island."

A shiver runs down your back as you remember the final words of your grandfather that day.

"That back bedroom, the southwest one, is inhabited by one of those spirits to this day. In all the years I've lived here no one has ever been able to sleep there through the night. It's my guess that it's the spirit of someone who was murdered out here. But . . . who knows. You never can tell."

Turn to the next page.

52

Ever since that time you have wanted to investigate these burial mounds. You know digging them up wouldn't be right, and you have no intention of doing that. But in light of your encounter with the voice, spending some time alone by the mounds might give you some answers to your questions about what happened and about your grandfather's stories.

You feel a tingle in your bones. Now might be the right time to do it. On the other hand, maybe you should look for Jayme and Lantern and get home. They must be really worried about you.

If you decide to stay with the mounds for a while, turn to page 66.

If you decide to search for Jayme and Lantern, turn to page 93.

"It seems there's a saboteur around these parts," Kelly explains. "They say he's been hired to do us in. Could be competition from another steamer company, could be a plot to stop business on the lake. Could be some kind of loony on the loose. You go and hang around, see what you can find out, okay?"

"I'll do my best," you answer.

You leave the boat, head up to the hotel, and mingle among the crowd for a while. Later you attach yourself to some of the kitchen help. Unfortunately, you come up with nothing. Everything seems to be fine and normal. No one mentions any trouble, any saboteurs or crazies. It's just a pleasant summer afternoon in 1890.

Turn to the next page.

54

That night, as you are about to return to the *Ticonderoga*, a fire breaks out—the one you read about that destroyed the hotel many years ago. The flames rush across the porch roof, through the windows, and up into the attics, exploding with a vengeance.

The wooden hotel becomes a smoldering ruin within a matter of hours. You watch helplessly as the *Ticonderoga* steams out into the lake. It's time for you to head back home.

Turn to the next page.

56

Heading through the woods, you suddenly encounter cold rain and fog! You keep on going until you reach the porch of the house on the north end. Once inside, you discover Jayme and Lantern curled up on one of the couches in front of a roaring fire. The old TV set is turned to a baseball game, and the reception is poor.

"Only thing that will come in," Jayme says to you as her way of greeting you. You nod slowly, realizing you're back in modern time.

Reaching into your pocket, you pull out the folded *New York Globe* from 1890. It is yellow with age, the only sign of your strange adventure.

The End

"We need to find our way back," you tell Jayme. "My dad always says caution is the better part of valor, which means don't stick your neck out if you don't have to. We're stuck in some kind of weird time loop. There's no sense in our working on a steamer—it's not going to get us any closer to home."

You scan the shoreline for some sign of a familiar path. The rocks are the same, but the place looks better kept, not at all like the wild island you know.

"Well, it's about time you came to your senses," Jayme says. "Let's get out of here. You lead the way."

Lantern bounces up, sniffing the air and ready for anything. The smell of breakfast from the hotel has made its way over to you. It suddenly dawns on you how hungry you are. It feels like breakfast was ages ago; however, now is not the time for a snack break, you realize.

"Follow me," you announce, leading Jayme and Lantern to shore.

Turn to the next page.

58

"Hey, you two, where are you going? We need you aboard the *Ticonderoga*," the captain shouts, throwing his apple core into the water. "Chances like this don't come your way too often, you know."

Ignoring him, the three of you duck into the trees. Soon you find yourself on a beautifully manicured path leading to the heart of the island. Several people pass you in horse-drawn carriages, but they take no notice of you. It's really strange seeing this mixture of past and present. You're still not sure what to make of it all.

Turn to page 25.

You give in to your feelings and stay where you are, deciding, out of curiosity, to go along for the ride. Lantern's mournful bark drifts farther and farther away, becoming more and more indistinct as the memory passes.

The silvery voice changes its tone once again. Now it is music, entirely new to your ears. It feeds a hunger inside you, calming you.

Your attention turns to the light figure. Before your eyes the figure grows until it is your size. It now has golden hair, and its face is the color of copper, with a luster that reflects the sun. You gaze within its eyes, which seem to radiate a warmth and a depth of understanding that surround you with a feeling of well-being.

"You have made some wise choices. I congratulate you from all of us here in the future," the figure says calmly.

"What do you mean, the 'future'?" you ask. "Who are you? What do you want with me?" A growing sense of fear rises within you. Hesitantly, you take two steps back. The figure hovers above the ground, smiling. The smile seems to grow in intensity, spreading like a ray of light.

Turn to page 102.

Suddenly you feel a tap on your shoulder. Turning, you see a face not unlike your own smiling back at you. The Indian is about your age and is standing alongside three others of varying ages: a baby, someone middle-aged, and a person who is old and wizened, with white hair and fragile limbs. They all look similar, clearly part of the same family and lineage.

"Would you like to join us?" one of them asks. Their smiles inspire you with confidence.

Turn to page 13.

62

The cave is narrow and dark. A thick layer of leaves and pine needles covers the floor.

"Yikes! What's that?" Jayme screams.

"Bats. Be cool; they're no problem," you say reassuringly.

Lantern comes up from behind you, startling you at first. You can just barely make him out in this darkness. You hold your breath, trying to stop your beating heart from jumping out of your mouth.

"Don't worry. We're safe in here," you say, hardly convincing even yourself.

"Let's go deeper," Jayme suggests.

"Might as well," you respond.

The three of you move forward slowly. The ground slopes under you at a fairly steep angle. Suddenly the cave opens up.

"Look! Light! But how in the world . . . ?" you ask with astonishment.

Turn to page 101.

"You stay here. I'll go check," you say to Jayme cautiously.

Reaching the edge of the cove, where the cliffs drop off down to the water, you see the source of the sound. There at anchor lies a 35-foot white and blue sloop. The Canadian flag, with its red maple leaf, flies from the stern. Aboard is a middle-aged couple wearing windbreakers and baseball caps. They are cooking on a charcoal grill suspended from the stern rail. A radio blasts out old sixties tunes. You see this a lot in the summer, when boats put into the cove to picnic and spend the night. These people, you guess, are probably late-season, hard-core sailors who must have been forced in here by the storm. You have never been so happy to see boat people in your cove before!

"Hey," you shout, waving. "Can we come onboard?"

Turn to page 19.

64

The boat is sitting in the water about 20 yards off the end of the pier. It is painted black, with a gold stripe from bow to stern. Lights below deck glow through the row of portholes. Aft of the stern is a small launch, big enough for several people. It rocks gently in the protected water of the small harbor.

"Wow! That's a big one. It was probably driven over by the storm," you say out loud. A strange fear descends upon you like winter darkness; you're not sure why. Maybe it's the sudden appearance of the boat. Maybe it's the strange feeling that has just come over you that there is no one aboard this boat. Or maybe it's just the culmination of your whole day.

Cautiously you retreat from the pier, hoping that if there is anyone aboard, they haven't seen you. You wish Jayme and Lantern were with you right now. You also wish that you were back home, instead of out here on Providence Island.

You leave the pier and gain the cover of a row of bushes that provides a shield from the harbor. You snake behind them, along the edge of the harbor, until you are not more than 20 yards from the power cruiser. The boat bristles with electronic gear, a mass of aerials sprouting from the cabin roof. There are no registration numbers on the bow, and no flag or pennant on the stern. This doesn't strike you as a good sign.

Turn to page 113.

Curiosity wins out; you decide to stay with the Indian burial mounds for a while.

There are more than twenty of these graves. You've always wanted to study them, to see if they form any pattern, perhaps a cross or an X or something like that. Now's your chance.

Slowly you move from mound to mound, looking carefully at each one, brushing the leaves and pine needles aside to see if there is anything more you can learn about them.

Go on to the next page.

There doesn't seem to be any apparent pattern to the placement, at least not from your vantage point. Then an idea hits you. You need to change your perspective. Why not climb a tree and get an aerial view?

The ancient oak beckons you. Moments later you are at its mammoth side, staring up into the gnarled branches that have mostly shed their summer's leaves.

"How am I going to get up there?" you ask yourself out loud, staring up at the first branch, which looms an impossible ten to twelve feet away.

Your dilemma is soon solved by your discovery of what appear to be steps cut into the side of the old trunk. They are faint but definite.

Turn to page 75.

68

The sun begins to break through the thick cloud cover, and the warming rays drift down through the pines in shafts of light. Looking around, you now see some familiar landmarks: to the right, an oak tree your dad has told you is over three hundred years old, and straight ahead a large rock formation that marks the beginning of the north end of the island.

"Okay, I know where I am," you announce to yourself. This is the part of the island known as the Indian Burial Ground.

You make out several six-foot-long humps on the ground rumored to be Indian graves from long ago. You remember the first time you heard about them, when you were about seven years old. Your grandfather was walking the trails of the island with you talking about its history. You can hear his voice to this day:

"Hundreds of years ago, long before the Europeans came to this continent, the Indians roamed these parts. Game was abundant, and the Indians traveled easily on the lake by canoe. The Great Spirits of the mountains and the lake looked favorably upon these people. For the most part they were friendly and not at all warlike as some would lead you to believe."

Turn to page 51.

70

The flames roar as they quickly spread over the dry wooden house. They scale the walls, burning the old pine beams that support the roof.

"We're finished!" you cry out to Stilton.

"No you're not," shouts Jayme, emerging from the secret passage behind the chimney. She cuts the ropes quickly and easily, setting the two of you free.

"Let's get out of here," you say.

"Hurry!" Stilton agrees.

Your arm still hurts, but you do your best to ignore it for now.

The sound of engines, deep and powerful, calls your attention to the harbor. The black boat slips its mooring and heads out onto the lake until it disappears into the fog and mist.

"Stilton," you ask in a demanding tone, "what is going on?"

"We're safe now," he says. "That's all that matters."

"Not so fast," you say. "You're not getting off that easy."

Turn to page 38.

"We might as well just wait and see if anything happens," you say to Jayme and Lantern.

"Who do you think they are?" Jayme asks.

"I don't know. There's just something about the boat that makes me nervous." The more you talk the more you frighten yourself with the prospect of dealing with whoever is onboard that boat.

Standing in the dripping rain, you feel a chill settling in your bones. But soon your suspicions are rewarded. Four people dressed in dark sweaters and dungarees come onto the deck. They carry with them what appear to be weapons. Another man, short and with a huge head, emerges on deck. He is carrying a small, rectangular box. He snaps out some orders to the others; unfortunately you can't make out what he is saying. They climb in the launch and head for shore.

Lantern, for whatever reason, lets out a loud fierce howl.

"Cool it," you whisper as fiercely as you can, giving his collar a yank. But it is too late.

Turn to page 105.

72

Waves can kick up on Lake Champlain in a matter of minutes. Frequently they build up to three, four, even five feet high; and the wind can easily hit up to thirty to thirty-five knots at a clip. Needless to say, you must be careful on the lake at all times.

Over the years, your dad has taught you a lot about the lake. One thing is that if you're going out, it's always a good idea to bring someone else along. With this in mind, you call up your friend Jayme who lives down the road. You like her, but she's not much of an adventurer. Still, having Jayme along would probably be a good idea. Besides, she's good company.

You dial Jayme's number. The telephone rings several times. You are about to hang up when she finally answers.

"The lake? Today? Right now? I don't know, the weather looks iffy," she responds to your proposal to go out to the island.

"Don't worry, it'll be fine. Haven't you always wanted to investigate those Indian burial mounds on the north end? Now's the perfect time. There'll be nobody around to bother us."

You wait for her response. You are sure she will come; the prospect of investigating burial mounds with entice her.

"Well, okay. But we'll turn back if it gets stormy, right?" Jayme warns.

"You bet," you reply, plunging your fist into the air victoriously.

Turn to page 7.

There is something very special about this spot and this very moment in time. It is as if you are connected to the past in some strange, unexplainable way. You want to squeeze yourself through the slit in the rocks and see what you can discover in the cave.

On the other hand, you've been separated from Jayme and Lantern for quite some time. You have to take them into consideration, too. They're probably frantic with worry by now, convinced that something has happened to you. In fact, they're probably calling the police. Oh, no! The last thing you need is for the police or the Coast Guard to go out searching for you. You'll really be in trouble then.

What should you do? If you look for Jayme and Lantern first, you can always go back to the cave.

If you decide to go back and find Jayme and Lantern first, turn to page 82.

If you decide to stay and search the cave, turn to page 22.

Lifting a foot to the first step and reaching up with your hands, you push off the ground, carefully scaling your way to the first branch. Your heartbeat increases, and your mouth becomes drier. As you stand on the branch, you steady yourself, then mount the second and third branches easily until you are more than twenty-five feet above the ground, staring down on the mounds.

"Hey, it's an arrow!" you shout. "An arrow pointing north."

You look to the immediate north of the mounds at a jumble of black rock left there by glaciers during the Pleistocene ice age, over eleven thousand years ago. You have seen the rocks before, but you never gave them much thought.

Turn to page 43.

Looking at the semi-deflated Zodiac now awash on the shore, you wonder what you're going to say to your father to explain this.

"Well, let's get some shelter."

You turn around to talk with Jayme, but she's gone. "Hey, Jayme, where are you? Lantern, go find Jayme, will you . . ." But Lantern, you realize, isn't anywhere to be found either.

"Okay, you two. You want to play games, we'll play games. But let's get dry first," you say loudly.

No one answers you. The fog and the trees soak up the sound of your voice, and nothing comes back. Cold and wet, you realize your body is shaking. You move across the slippery rocks, clawing up the sandy embankment toward the line of trees. An oppressive quiet surrounds you, deadening your brain and your thoughts. "Gosh, I'm beat. Really beat," you say.

"I don't blame you," an unfamiliar voice answers with a menacing tone. It seems to be coming from over by the trees. You freeze in your steps, your right hand gripping the wet branch of a birch tree for support

"You'd better come this way," the voice says. This time it sounds thinner and farther away.

The rough water is behind you, the forest in front. You are alone now. Time seems to hang in the balance, suspended by the tension of your indecision.

Turn to page 27.

"Count me in," you announce to the captain, looking at Jayme for some sign of agreement.

"Me too, I guess," she says dejectedly.

"Fine, sign your name in the book up on the bridge and ask for First Officer Kelly. Glad to have you aboard," he says. "Off you go. You won't regret this."

"I hope you know what you've gotten us into," Jayme announces with a disgruntled air.

"Well, we're better off than we were in that storm in the Zodiac. Look."

You gaze around. It's a sunny summer day. The temperature is in the low eighties, you judge, wiping a thin line of sweat from your brow.

For lack of a better option, you head for the bridge of the steamer and sign yourselves on as crew.

Turn to page 94.

The house isn't far away. Moments later you reach the phone, lift it, and begin to dial 911.

"I wouldn't do that if I were you," comes a thickly-accented voice. You respond immediately, calmly putting the phone back down. Jayme lets out an audible gasp. Slowly the two of you turn and face your adversary.

Before you stands a middle-aged man who looks like he lives in the woods. His dark hair is a tangled mess, and his overall appearance is equally unkempt. In his hand, he holds a black revolver. There is no emotion on his face, just a look of fierce determination.

"Very good," he says. "Now the two of you, come over here." He motions with the revolver to the center of the large room. Light from the old wagon-wheel chandelier circles him in a wreath of amber. He moves with short, jerky steps. You and Jayme do as the man says.

Lantern, however, hunkers down on the floor and emits a low growl. The man reels around, stepping back slowly.

Turn to page 98.

80

The thought of Lantern, combined with the sound of his howl, helps you to break away from this vision. With some regret you begin to pull yourself back from the shining light resting in front of you.

Your footsteps once again are heavy and unsure; they seem to stick in the flowers, which slowly change into mud and rocks.

At last you are out of the forest! A sense of despair descends upon you as the previous feeling of complacency evaporates. It is now cold, wet, and windy once again.

Turn to page 114.

Your chances, you figure, might be better if you climbed up on the roof. They'd never think of looking for you there, and you'll be able to keep an eye on them.

Gingerly you mount the rickety ladder, rung by rung, past the porch roof first, then stepping carefully onto the main roof.

Lantern, anxious to stay with you, tries his best to climb the ladder but fails miserably.

"Stay!" you command in your best whisper. He looks ready to bark, but you shake your head and point to the bushes. Obediently he turns around and hides behind them.

Now comes the tricky part. There are places on the roof where the wood has rotted; one false step and you will join the party inside the house without being invited.

Step by step you carefully climb the roof, creep along the ridge, and skirt around the chimney until you are directly over the main living room.

"Forget those kids. They don't know anything anyway. We will be gone long before they can return with any help," says a voice in a thick accent.

"What do we do now, Ludwig?" says another voice.

This second voice is strangely familiar. You wonder who it could be when suddenly . . .

Turn to page 106.

82

You decide that it would be wisest to go back and find Jayme and Lantern, then return and explore the cave with their help. After all, the cave has been here for a long time; it isn't going anywhere.

You hurry off in the direction of your parents' house, certain that your friend and dog will be waiting there for you.

When you get there, you find Jayme and Lantern in the living room. Jayme is huddled over the telephone, while Lantern looks sad and mournful, his head hanging low.

"Hey, it's me!" you shout, but neither one looks up. Jayme continues to speak into the telephone.

"Yes, I'm quite sure no one else came ashore besides us," she says. "No . . . we haven't searched the water, it's too windy and foggy out. When can you be here?"

You walk up to Jayme and tap her on the shoulder. No response. You slap her on top of her head—still no response.

"Jayme, Lantern, it's me! Hey, what's wrong with you two?" you shout, beginning to get frantic.

Jayme hangs up the phone. "I can't believe it," she says. "My best friend drowned. I just can't believe it."

Turn to page 40.

"I'm with you," you say to Jayme, deciding to turn around and head back. You know that it's okay to give up. Your dad has always stressed that there is no shame in turning back, whether it be on a lake, a mountain, anywhere. "Know your limits," he says.

Jayme mutters something in reply, but you can't hear her. She grips the bowline. Like you, she is soaked to the skin. The waves are relentless, and it's getting cold fast. Lantern looks at you with the gaze he reserves for food begging.

"Okay, here we go!" you say, trying to convince yourself as much as Jayme. Slowly you push the handle of the engine to starboard, initiating a big turn in the rough waves and swells. The bow comes around, then hesitates for a moment as the wind catches it and tries to push it back. You increase power, feeling the bow banging against the waves. The Zodiac bucks but makes headway in its long turn.

For a moment you are facing right into the teeth of the wind, which has shifted and is now coming from due south. The clouds have lowered; you can no longer make out the island or the shore.

Turn to page 18.

84

As if waking from a dream, you find yourself back at the entrance of the cave, staring into its darkness. It is now time for you to join Jayme and Lantern.

Hurrying through the woods, you still hear the faint sound of chanting. It gives you comfort and brings you pleasure.

Soon you reach your parents' summer house, located on the height of land near the middle of the island. The sun is just setting over the Adirondacks. You can smell wood smoke coming from one of the big chimneys.

"Jayme! Lantern! It's me! I'm back!" you yell.

Together they both come racing out of the house onto the big porch.

"Where have you been?" Jayme says. "I've been scared to death about you. We searched the entire island." There is relief in her voice.

"You wouldn't believe it. I've been—" But you stop yourself. How can you ever explain all that has happened to you? No one would believe it.

You promise yourself that when it feels right, you will take Jayme to the burial grounds and the cave that opened up a whole world for you. Deep within yourself you can still sense the faint rhythms of chanting. Somehow, you are certain you will know when it is time to return.

The End

There is something about a ringing telephone that has always bugged you. Instinct says this call probably spells trouble. But the ring tugs at your conscience. Against your better judgment, you answer it.

"Hello," you say cautiously, ready for bad news.

There is a pause, a sound of electronic beeping, and then a familiar voice comes on the line. You can't believe it; it's Belinda Grist, of all people.

"I'm just calling to make sure you're all right," she says in her syrupy do-good voice. "Are you?"

For a fleeting moment you think about letting out a gasp, feigning cardiac arrest, and choking out your thanks that somebody has finally called. But you let the idea go almost as quickly as it forms.

"Fine," you say. "Couldn't be better. Thanks for calling, but I gotta be going now." You quickly hang up the phone, as if it were a poisonous snake ready to strike. Relieved, you slump into a chair.

Turn to page 21.

You are lured by the sounds. Setting your fears aside, you move over to the clearing with quick cautious steps.

"No way!" you exclaim out loud at what lies before you—a huge oval-shaped clearing, and hundreds of American Indians! Some wear deer antlers fixed to their heads; others have white wings attached to their backs. Another group wears foxtails. Beyond them lie people with their backs painted to look like scaly fish.

Together they are dancing, chanting, and singing. On the sides are hundreds more, seated and looking on with respectful silence. You move closer, keeping a safe distance to avoid being discovered.

Turn to page 61.

With a nod to Jayme, you put the motor in gear, lean the mixture, and cruise out of the harbor onto the open lake. Providence Island lies in the distance.

The first set of waves rolls the rubber boat a bit to starboard, but it bobs over the waves like a cork. The bow picks up spray and sloshes Jayme, who sits on the port side. She pulls her scarf tightly around her dark hair and girds herself against the next wave. She doesn't have to wait long. Two big ones slide over the bow.

You increase your speed, ride on top of the next wave, then down the trough, picking up power as you mount the next one. It's great fun, just like riding a horse, or skiing, or flying. You don't fear the water, and the waves are challenging. You find it thrilling.

Now and then you look at the sky, then get your bearing on the island about a mile and a half away. You can't go any faster, not in these waters. You have to take it slow and easy, figuring each group of waves as they come, slowly edging toward the island. Jayme is soaked and looks totally miserable. She is hanging on to the bowline as if her life depended on it.

Turn to page 10.

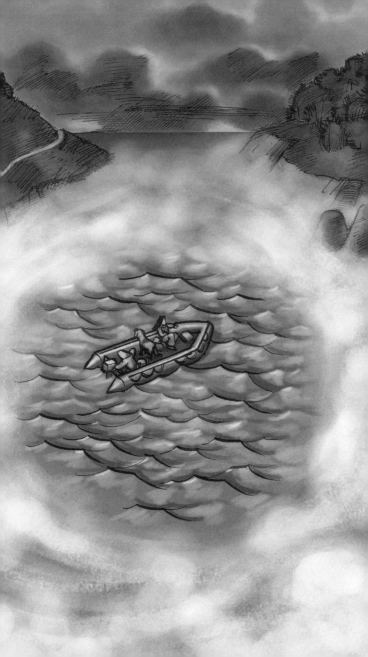

Suddenly you are broadsided by three huge waves. You struggle into your life vest, then turn your attention to the motor. No luck! You try all the standard procedures: you check the fuel, reset the fuel line, pull the start cord, and mess with the adjustments and settings. Nothing. Not even a kick.

The two paddles you keep in the boat are of little help. The waves continue to pound, moving you along.

"We'll be killed!" Jayme shouts.

"We'll be all right," you answer nervously.

You judge that the Zodiac is headed toward the Gut, a narrow channel between the island and the mainland. The Gut is famous for rough waves. You remember a powerboat several summers ago that lost its engine in a similar storm and was driven right through the Gut, out into the center of the lake. You and your dad stood by helplessly, watching the boat and its frantic crew as it was swept along by the current. The Coast Guard eventually picked them up and towed the boat back in to safety.

Turn to the next page.

That was in the summer, and there weren't any clouds or fog around to complicate navigation. You, on the other hand, are lost in fog; and what's worse, it's fall, not summer. The weather is bad, and the lake is practically deserted. Even the Coast Guard has reduced the number of its routine patrols. The last radio transmission you heard was a while ago, but it estimated the water temperature for most of the lake to be around 52 degrees Fahrenheit, a temperature humans can't survive in for more than a half hour.

As best as you can judge, you are now in the Gut or close to it. Either way, you're headed for the broad center of the lake. Once there, you'll really be in big trouble.

Turn to page 39.

Reluctantly, you leave the Indian burial mounds and head back through the woods in search of Jayme and Lantern. When you reach your parents' house in the middle of the island, you find, much to your surprise and dismay, that no one is there, nor are there any signs that your friend and dog have been there. You write a short note saying that you are okay and tack it up on the bulletin board next to the telephone. You then throw the main switch, turning the electricity on. It's family practice to always turn the power off when you leave the house. Now you can turn on a few lights. It tends to be dark inside the big house because of the pines outside that block the sunlight.

Changing into some dry clothes stored in one of the bedrooms, you set out once again in search of Jayme and Lantern.

A strange silence seems to have taken over the island, as if there is not another living creature around besides you.

"Hey, Jayme! Lantern!" you shout from the bottom of your lungs, but no one answers.

You follow the path down to the big concrete pier that juts out into the lake from the little harbor. There is no sign of anything but fog. However, it does seem to be lifting, and the wind has died down considerably. Sunshine breaks through the low clouds, revealing a huge powerboat!

Turn to page 64.

Two hours later, you and Jayme wear the blue shirts of the steamship *Ticonderoga*. The shirts have red anchors embroidered on the front.

Your first job is to swab the decks. This wasn't exactly your idea of life on the lake, but then again, you didn't plan on any of this for your day off.

"Hey, you there, work harder," a surly man says. "This ain't no party. At least, for you it ain't." The man wears a whistle around his neck. You guess that he is the second mate in charge of deck-hands.

You look around. Lantern has slunk off to the side of the steamer, out of the way of people and officers.

"I don't like this," Jayme says.

Turn to page 99.

96

"Hang on, Jayme. We're in for a rough ride," you say. You see her wet face looking up at you, a mixture of hope and fear written across it You feel sorry and a little guilty that you got her into this mess in the first place.

You've got to stay calm, you try and convince yourself. All right, so what if you're stranded on a deserted lake in a small boat with no motor. Just because you're trapped in a huge storm with no visibility and no one knows that you're out here isn't cause for alarm. Okay, so your case won't hold up in court; that's no reason to panic.

There is some consolation. If you are going to be trapped in a storm, the Zodiac is the best of all possible boats. It won't sink. You've also got good old Lantern with you. Who knows, he may come in handy.

"What do we do now?" Jayme asks dejectedly.

"Well, I figure we're in the Gut by now. We might as well hang on and let the lake take us where it wants to." You flash Jayme a forced smile, trying to reassure her.

Turn to page 32.

"How much is not much?" you ask.

"Pushy youngster, aren't you?" the captain says, grinning at the two of you. "Well, I'm a good judge of character and a generous, fair man by nature. Let's say, oh . . . two dollars." He smiles, waiting for your reply.

"Only two dollars an hour?" Jayme says in disbelief. "Starting wage at a fast-food place is five-fifty for kitchen help with no experience."

"An hour?" the captain balks. "Are you mad? I'm talking two dollars a week, and all you can eat, of course. Two dollars an hour? Why, I've never heard of such foolishness." He pulls out an apple and bites into it with a crackle, giving you a chuckle.

You have no idea what is going on, much less how you got here. You and Jayme look at each other blankly, unable to come up with even a theory as to how you wound up back in time. However, strange as it might seem, this could be an interesting opportunity, you think. You were looking for some adventure. The more you think about it, though, the more you wonder if maybe you should slip away and try and figure out a way back home to the present before you get stuck in this time warp.

If you decide to take the job, turn to page 77.

If you decide to find your way back, turn to page 57.

"I see that this dog is going to be trouble," the man says. "I'll just have to take care of that."

Suddenly Lantern charges, leaping on top of the man with his full body weight. The two smack the floor like professional wrestlers.

"Come on, Lantern! Run for it!" you shout.

You and Jayme dash for the rear porch door, making your way outside. Lantern follows, leaving the strange man in a lump on the floor.

"Follow me!" you gasp breathlessly.

With an instinct for survival, the three of you run helter-skelter through the woods in the direction of the Indian burial mounds. It doesn't take long for you to get there. You hear shouts coming from the direction of the house. It's only a matter of time before you'll be caught!

"Quick, in here," you say to Jayme and Lantern, pointing to the rocks and the entrance to the cave.

"Not me. I hate caves," Jayme says. "Bats, snakes, spiders!"

"No problem. I'll just stir them up. That way they'll be ready for you when they finally get here and you come running in after me," you say, entering the cave.

"Wait for me!" Jayme cries, following fast on your heels.

Turn to page 62.

"Hang in there," you reassure Jayme. "This could be interesting. Just wait until tonight."

"Not me, I'm getting out of here," she says with a worried look on her face. "I'll bet if we just walk up the path to the house on the north end, we'll walk right out of this time machine. You with me?"

You think for a minute. "Go for it," you tell Jayme. "I'll meet you there tomorrow at dawn. I'm going to see what I can find out around here. Do me a favor, take Lantern with you. Hey, good luck," you add, then return to swabbing the deck.

"Same to you," Jayme says, sneaking off the boat with Lantern and heading up the path through the woods.

Turn to page 20.

Creeping toward the light, the three of you come across an old man sitting by a fire. The light reveals a large chamber with a high ceiling.

"Well, good afternoon. I've been expecting you. Would you like some tea?"

"Who are you?" you ask, unsure how there could be someone living in this cave. And from the looks of it, he has been here for quite some time. There are a bed, pots and pans, several kerosene lanterns, some books, even an old beach chair. It seems quite comfortable, for a cave.

"I'm just a friend. A friend of the world, you might say," the old man says cryptically.

Turn to page 42.

"You have joined your future time," the figure says. "Humans are outside the true realm of time. Whether they know it or not, they spend their lives waiting to get back to the real time."

The figure smiles once again, enveloping you in its light.

Something inside you begins to question the intentions of this figure. You grow skeptical. "Sounds like you know quite a lot about what we want and what we need. On whose authority do you speak, anyway?"

The figure is taken aback by your tone. "Do not question the experience," it says, trying to recapture your devotion once again. "Remember, you made the decision to come. You stepped outside your circle of life, we didn't take you. We merely guided you, helping you to make the right choice over the wrong one."

Talk of right and wrong begins to worry you. Your parents taught you never to speak in absolutes. You are beginning to distrust the whole situation.

"Where am I?" you demand. You hear Lantern's bark once again in the distance; it pulls at you, calling you back.

Turn to page 45.

"Swim!" you command. "Let's go for it."

Jayme gives you a look as if to say what choice do I have? Lantern, on the other hand, is doing just fine, paddling along, following your lead.

The water temperature is probably around fifty degrees. You know that you've got to hurry and get to shore or you'll soon die of hypothermia. If your body temperature drops too far, it won't come back up. Probably twenty minutes in this water is about all one can take. The cold water is no problem for Lantern; his fur coat acts like a wet suit.

"Swim!" you manage to shout again between strokes. Jayme flounders a bit, but she's a strong swimmer.

Stroke after stroke you continue on, the waves beating against you. You continue to swim until you see the white hull of a boat—it's coming right toward you.

You and Jayme wave and scream with all your might.

The sound of the motor buries your screams; you pray that the boat doesn't plough right over you. You're in luck—they've spotted you!

Turn to page 28.

104

You decide to stay down on the ground, hidden by a clump of old raspberry bushes and weeds. Lantern snuggles in as close to you as possible. It's comforting to have him with you, just in case.

Just then you see someone you know—it's Mr. Stilton, your family's accountant. Your parents have done business with him for years. He's been over to the house many times.

Hey, wait a minute, you think to yourself. I remember hearing something about Stilton. Didn't Dad say that he couldn't be trusted anymore? Something about Stilton filling his pockets with other people's money.

You are brought back to the dangerous reality of the moment by a scraping sound coming from the wall in front of you.

"Jayme? Is that you?" you ask in a half-whisper.

"Yeah, it's me. How do I get out of here? It's really grungy. I can't see a thing."

You think hard before you reply. There is a way out other than the entrance. Then you remember.

"Jayme, there's a trapdoor on the floor. It's not far from where you entered. You'll have to feel around for it."

"Where does it lead?" she asks.

Turn to page 50.

The launch stops, and the people aboard scan the shoreline until they fix their gaze in your direction.

"We should get out of here," you whisper to Jayme, but she doesn't need the suggestion. She's already up the path, running toward the house. You decide to stay where you are for the moment. Lantern, loyal dog that he is, remains at your side, hunkering down close to you.

You watch in silence as the launch comes alongside the pier and those aboard jump out onto the narrow concrete walkway.

"To the house! Don't let them escape!" shouts the short man with the huge head.

You hope that Jayme remembers the secret passage behind the chimney in the dining room. It leads from the old part of the house into the newer addition built about thirty years ago.

The group runs up the path coming within two or three yards of where you are hiding. An idea suddenly occurs to you: you can swim to the boat and take control of it!

On the other hand, Jayme may be in trouble. Perhaps you should sneak up to the house behind these men and see if she needs help.

If you decide to take control of their boat, turn to page 44.

If you decide to sneak up to the house, turn to page 109.

106

With a cracking snap, the roof gives way underneath you, sending you slamming down onto the floor of the living room.

"My arm!" you scream, holding your arm in pain.

"That's nothing compared to what I'm about to do to you," says the short man with the big head and the thick accent.

"No! I won't allow it. Leave the kid alone," says the man with the familiar voice. "This one knows nothing."

Looking up, you are shocked to see your family's accountant, Frank Stilton.

"Mr. Stilton, what are you doing here?" you blurt out, clutching your arm.

"Shut up, kid!" Ludwig commands.

Stilton moves over, protecting you.

"You have chosen sides poorly, Stilton," Ludwig says. "Tie the two of them up!" he says to the others. "Then we'll set fire to this place."

Moments later, you and Stilton are bound hand and foot, back to back, seated on two chairs. The henchmen then strike several matches and swiftly set the fire.

Turn to page 70.

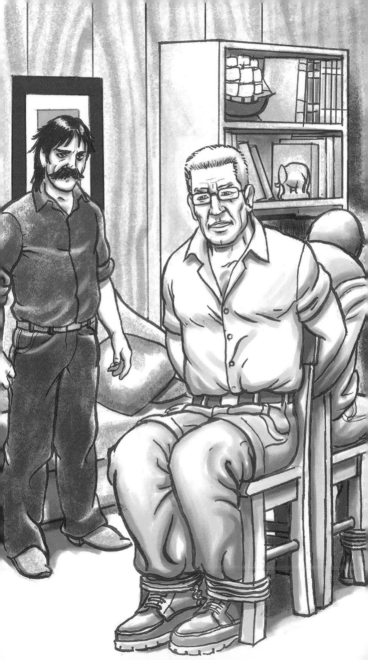

108

Cautiously you move forward, painfully aware that each step brings you closer and closer to the unknown. Somehow you know instinctively that your feet are actually carrying you forward into another dimension of time and space. Fear and curiosity struggle within you as the voice leads the way.

"Do not be afraid. We will not hurt you," the voice says, floating on the wind. There is a quality to it that now begins to soothe you, eroding your fear. You walk through the pine forest easily, noticing that the branches don't touch you, and the damp rain and fog no longer affect you. Everything feels dreamlike, and you are comforted by a growing sense of light and warmth.

"Not much longer. Keep walking," the voice encourages.

Turn to page 31.

"I'd better see if Jayme is okay," you say to Lantern.

Taking a shortcut, you arrive at the side of the house just as the others are entering through the front door. Jayme is nowhere to be seen. You just hope she remembered the secret passage.

A ladder leans against the roof of the back wing, left there from last summer when you and your dad fixed the roof.

What to do? Maybe you should climb onto the roof and spy on the men from there. They won't be able to see you. On the other hand, if you were found, escape would be difficult. Maybe you should just stay on the ground and see what you can do.

If you decide to climb up onto the roof, turn to page 81.

If you decide to stay on the ground, turn to page 104.

As you get closer, to your astonishment, you make out a huge paddle wheeler tied up to a dock protruding from the rocky shoreline of Providence Island.

"What in the world is that?" Jayme shouts.

Instinctively you head the Zodiac toward shore, pulling up alongside the huge steamer. Painted on the hull, you read the name *Ticonderoga*.

"Good gosh! Do you see what I see?" you ask Jayme, pointing at the name of the steamer.

"I'm not so sure," she replies. "Look over there!"

Together you stare at the figures on the dock and the large carriage loaded with baggage and supplies, which is moving up a path that leads toward a huge white hotel!

"I must be seeing things," you say, shocked to your very core.

You recall pictures you have seen of the island from the 1800s. There used to be a hotel on the southern end. Steamers made the 120-mile trip up north to the Richelieu River and Canada. Providence Island was a stopover point for passengers, and the hotel was famous throughout the region. Dancing, great food, and boating on the lake attracted visitors until one day when the hotel mysteriously burned down in a blaze that could be seen for miles around.

"This is really weird," Jayme says.

You nod in agreement, unable to speak.

Turn to page 48.

"Who's there?" a frightened voice whispers from the bushes ahead of you. It's Jayme! She's okay!

"It's me. Where's Lantern?" you reply. With that, Lantern comes bounding over to you, licking your face and wagging his tail, all excited to see you.

"It's you! I thought you were dead," Jayme cries with relief. "We were searching for you up at the north end. Let's get back."

You reach out and grab Jayme by the elbow. "Not yet. Look," you say, pointing to the black powerboat on the water.

"Whose is it?" Jayme asks.

"I don't know, but something tells me it's trouble," you reply.

"Let's call for some help," Jayme suggests.

You consider going up to the house and using the phone, but something warns you against it

"Maybe we should keep an eye on them for a while," you say. "Who knows, they may be harmless. Maybe they're Canadians who got caught in the storm."

Turn to page 116.

114

Suddenly you find yourself back in the woods near the Zodiac. You are lying on the ground, exhausted and shivering with cold as the rain falls on you.

Your eyes focus, and you hear the sounds of Jayme and Lantern.

"You're alive!" Jayme cries.

Lantern licks your face, bringing you to your feet. "Cut it out, Lantern," you say. "I'm all right, I'm all right."

"I thought you were dead," Jayme says. We made it to the house, but you never came. I looked all over, but I couldn't find you. It's a good thing Lantern was here. He was able to track you down. Come, I built a fire. You'll be warm in no time."

Lantern gives you one last lick, then the three of you start up the trail to the house. You can't remember everything that happened to you, but in a way you're lucky. There are some things you probably shouldn't experience until you are really ready. Maybe this was one of them. You feel as if you've just been enchanted, as if you've been wrapped up in the plot of the kind of movie you haven't liked since you were very young. Anyway, what a day off!

The End

116

"Beats me," Jayme says, shaking her head with a shrug of her shoulders.

There's no real right or wrong decision, you realize, in this situation. You can either follow your gut, exercise caution, and see what happens. Or you can call for help and hope it arrives before whatever happens, happens.

If you decide to go to the house and call for help, turn to page 78.

If you decide to wait and keep an eye on the boat, turn to page 71.

GLOSSARY

Adirondacks – A mountain range in the northeastern part of New York State, which is encompassed by the six-million-acre Adirondack State Park. Along with the mountains, the park contains thousands of streams and lakes—among them, Lake Placid, twice the site of the winter Olympics.

Automatic bailing – A design that allows for excess water in a boat to be pumped or suctioned out, eliminating the need for bailing buckets.

Cardiac arrest – When the heart suddenly stops beating.

Cumulus clouds – Dense, puffy clouds that often form in towers with flat bases. Cumulus clouds are formed lower in the atmosphere than some other types and are most common in warm, summery weather.

Green Mountains – Vermont's mountain range. The range is about 250 miles long and peaks with Mt. Mansfield, which is 4,393 feet tall. The Green Mountains are part of the Appalachian mountain system, which stretches the length of the United States' east coast.

Hypothermia – A physical condition in which the body temperature drops to below 95 degrees Fahrenheit and other body systems, such as metabolism, are affected. If the body temperature falls below 90 degrees, hypothermia can lead to death.

Lake Champlain – The sixth-largest body of fresh water in the United States. Lake Champlain divides the northern sections of Vermont and New York and extends into Canada. In 1998, the lake briefly became the country's sixth Great Lake, though this title was soon stripped due to public pressure.

Pleistocene – Also known as the Ice Age, the Pleistocene period began about 1.6 million years ago and ended about 10,000 years ago with the melting of large glaciers across much of the earth's land masses.

Richelieu River – The Canadian river that drains Lake Champlain. It stretches about 75 miles north of the lake and then drains into the much larger St. Lawrence River.

Solar house – A house that runs on heat and light from the sun. Solar panels collect the sun's energy and then turn it into heat and electricity. Solar energy is environmentally friendly because it does not result in pollution and is renewable, which means the supply naturally regenerates itself and is virtually impossible to deplete. Other sources of renewable energy are wind, water, and vegetation.

Westerlies – West-to-east air currents found in the middle latitudes of both hemispheres. Westerlies typically blow from the southwest to the north in the northern hemisphere. They are known for the strength of their winds.

CREDITS

This book is the work of many people. R. A. Montgomery reviewed and edited the original manuscript, bringing it into the Internet age. Shannon Gilligan, Melissa Bounty, Susanne Pingree, and James Woodard at Chooseco LLC, and Kate McQuade, Marlene Stemple, Ellen Maxwell, and Julie Shattuck at Sundance Publishing, nursed it through various stages of editorial and artistic development. Stacey Hood at Big Eyedea Visual Design in Bigfork, Montana, was responsible for layout and design. Jim Wallace proofread and corrected the final words. Laura Sanderson kept everyone informed and on track. Gordon Troy performed the legal pirouettes that result in proper trademark and copyright protections. *A very special thanks to Wick Van Heuven, Sherry Litwack, Bob Laronga, and Judy Cooper.*

Illustrator: Marco Cannella was born in Ascoli Piceno, Italy, on September 29, 1972. Marco started his career in art as decorator and illustrator when he was a college student. He became a full-time professional in 2001 when he received the flag-prize for the "Palio della Quintana" (one of the most important Italian historical games). Since then, he has worked as illustrator for the Studio Inventario in Bologna. He has also worked as scenery designer for professional theater companies. He works for the production company ASP sril in Rome as character designer and set designer on the preproduction of a CG feature film. In 2004, he moved to Bangalore, India, to work full-time on this project as art director.

ABOUT THE AUTHOR

    R. A. MONTGOMERY has hiked in the Himalayas, climbed mountains in Europe, scuba-dived in Central America, and worked in Africa. He lives in France in the winter, travels frequently to Asia, and calls Vermont home. Montgomery graduated from Williams College and attended graduate school at Yale University and NYU. His interests include macro-economics, geo-politics, mythology, history, mystery novels, and music. He has two grown sons, a daughter-in-law, and two granddaughters. His wife, Shannon Gilligan, is an author and noted interactive game designer. Montgomery feels that the new generation of people under 15 is the most important asset in our world.

Visit us online at CYOA.com for games and other fun stuff, or to write to R. A. Montgomery!